The Three Books

First published in Great Britain in 2018 by Black Shuck Books

Cover design by WHITEspace
from "Temple of New York"
by Christopher Nevinson
Courtesy of the Cleveland Museum of Art

Set in Caslon by WHITEspace
www.white-space.uk

978-1-913038-23-6

The Three Books

by
Paul StJohn Mackintosh

BLACK
SHUCK
BOOKS

*Dedicated to the Cenobite Muse
who inspired this story*

Sophia Amory had always loved the written word, and the written word requited her. Books were her refuge from her lonely, neglected childhood in Worcester, Massachusetts, with her cold, indifferent mother and alcoholic, eventually abusive stepfather: Alice in Wonderland and Narnia in her childhood; Faulkner, Poe and Thoreau later on. Words became her escape ladder out of grim, stultifying backwoods New England. Loving books as she did, she inevitably fell in love with their creators, and pursued them with unflagging ardor through high school, then college, all the way to graduate school at NYU, with a major in Modern American Literature and minor in Critical Theory, distancing herself as far as she could from her past on the far side of the Harlem River.

All of Sophia's reading and studies primed her for the work, and the legend, of Desmond Carvill. No one had seen Carvill since his debut. All extant pictures of the poet predated his first collection: Carvill as an altar boy in Hell's Kitchen, Carvill a freshman at Columbia, Carvill onstage with Chris Burden, Carvill with William Burroughs, Carvill in London at the Wellcome Institute, at Little Sparta near Edinburgh with Ian Hamilton Finlay. Poem-fragments scribbled before his breakthrough held few hints of the brilliance to come – occasional glittering lines, buried in sub-Ginsbergian rants. Then this tagalong on the fringes of New York's pre-9.11 performance art scene suddenly emerged, fully formed, as a major poet, accessible enough to feature in Valentine's Day cards, yet deep and enigmatic enough to baffle scholars for over a decade, author of two sonnet cycles whose own genesis, as one-off art books rarely seen and never reproduced, was as remarkable and mystifying as their contents. Emerged – then disappeared. After his debut with *Daphnia*, Carvill dropped off the grid. There were occasional sightings, and rumors, Facebook groups and conspiracy theories about his motives for vanishing, hoax articles and spoofs; but genuine attested appearances, none.

Correspondence with Carvill, such as it was, went through an equally reclusive agent. Otherwise, he joined Salinger, Pynchon, and Bigfoot among America's literary cryptids. Until – and that was where Sophia came in – the publication of his third book, *The Tower*, showcasing a new style and, in most evaluations, a huge loss of form. Some critics speculated that the collection was a hoax, so drastic was the shift in approach and so inconsistent the resulting work, with its cryptic epigraph, "this is not my third book." The consensus was that either Carvill was just going through the motions, or someone else, for whatever reason, was doing it for him.

Sophia's breakthrough moment with Carvill came after her successful doctoral exam in the middle of her second year as an NYU post-grad, during the recovery phase from her latest bout of depression. She had struggled with the condition since her early teens, and preferred to ride her depressive episodes out, rather than try to treat them though therapy or medication, and during the recovery phase after each episode, her thoughts often started churning like a hamster on a wheel. Carvill's third book had been perplexing her just before her latest relapse. Snatches of Carvill's verse, details of his biography picked up from her doctoral exam, spun and wove together in her mind, until they gelled into a single, barely articulate form. Inspired, she sat up in bed, clicked on her reading lamp, and jotted down the few half-sentences that would form the topic for her PhD dissertation.

Traditional forms meant a lot to Sophia; so did word magic, and the enigmatic poet's masterworks oozed both, breeding a fascination that developed into an obsession. Sophia had never had much time for Beat bluster; Carvill, in contrast, used strict forms to sound abstracted, impersonal depths the Beats never had, yet he did that through passionate engagement with the body of the loved one. Or ones – the two celebrated muses of *Daphnia* and *Nyx*, the subjects of his two cycles of love sonnets, studied, researched, envied… and still as mysterious as Carvill's verse, and his own whereabouts.

She outlined her insight to her best friend at NYU, Gaye Kawasaki, as they sat together later the same morning for coffee outside a terrace cafe in Schwartz Plaza, under the Founder's Memorial. Gaye was West Coast Japanese, formed like something out of a Paul Auster story, small, oriental, elegant and clean-cut as her sharp, precise thought processes. This morning, she sported a fresh tattoo on her left shoulder, still under its protective sheath of saran wrap – a bird design, as far as Sophia could make out.

"What's that?" she asked her friend.

Gaye giggled, glancing down sidelong at the tat. "I've got a friend who's a tattoo apprentice, so I decided to give her a go. She just needs skin."

"It's permanent, though. You didn't mind?"

Gaye shrugged. "I chose the design. Besides, you only live once, right?" She sipped her latte, then refocused her cool brown gaze on Sophia. "So okay, hon, what's this big thing you wanted to tell me about?"

Sophia stumbled over her words at first, already imagining herself defending the topic in front of a sceptical faculty review board. But as she warmed to the theme, it came more and more easily, until she found herself almost gushing.

"You know that Carvill is a very tactile poet, very sensual," she explained. "Very few abstract ideas in his sonnets. That's one reason why ordinary readers pick up on him. Then look at his past track record in the performance art scene, and his earliest poems: very physical, even visceral. Everyone knows he wrote down his first verses *avant le motif,* right in front of his actual subject matter, in real time, almost like word portraiture. He even interviewed about that, before he went dark. And from there, he goes on to write a sonnet cycle that is basically a series of portraits of his lover, every aspect of her body and personality. And that first cycle is written as a single-copy artist's book, a work of art in itself, which somehow gets transcribed somewhere along the way, then disappears as completely as Carvill himself."

Gaye sucked her lip. "With you so far. Go on."

Sophia took a deep breath. "So what if we've been looking at this the wrong way? What if Carvill is fundamentally a visual or a plastic artist, not a poet at all? A sculptor, maybe? A book artist, certainly. There have been precedents. What if Carvill's unique handling of words stems from him treating them as sensual objects in their own right, not signs? What if the third book didn't work out precisely because it was his first attempt to write words as words, instead of sculpt them as things?"

Gaye gazed at her friend for and took a moment to consider. "Okay, sort of with you there. But if that's so, what does it say about Carvill's use of language? About language itself? Where are you going with this?"

"I don't know," Sophia admitted to Gaye, and to herself. "But think of song composition, with music and lyrics. Or William Blake's illuminated books. I think Carvill felt his way down to some Chomskyan deep layer underlying all language, through the physical substance of the written word. And I think that's why his work is so mysterious, and so powerful."

Gaye nodded. "You're going to have trouble proving it, though. Not that it's not a valid interpretation. But it's not really evidence-based. You're going to have to stack up a lot of proofs to make it stick. And of course, some kind of supporting comment from Carvill himself wouldn't hurt, but I guess that's not coming any time soon."

"The original art books are evidence," Sophia countered. "We're not talking regular published books here, or even manuscripts. These are one-offs. Works of art, made to be admired and treasured, not read. That suggests a pretty powerful commitment to the visual and tactile, don't you think?"

"Art books which, if the rumors are right, have never been seen since the poem texts were copied down from them, yeah?" Gaye pointed out. "Which may never even have existed. They've never been exhibited, never been photographed, only rumored. There's already enough doubt over the true authorship of Carvill's third book. What if his art books never existed either? Just the inspiration of some publicist trying to hype the Carvill legend?"

"So you think I'm going up a blind alley?" Sophia sniffed, a little brought down despite herself.

Gaye reached across the table and took her hand with a warm smile. "You know I'm your friend, hon. I'm only saying this to help you out. If I thought it couldn't work, I'd tell you, trust me."

Sophia gave a small nod and wan smile. "If I were you, I'd go after the art books," Gaye continued. "They may be easier to find than Carvill himself, if they do exist, and some publishing pros must have seen them to get the verse down on paper. There's your evidence, if you can find it."

"And if they don't exist?" Sophia asked, despite herself.

"Then if you can prove that, you have a win either way," Gaye chuckled. "You go, girl. This could make you."

Back in her room after that first meeting with Gaye, Sophia looked up George Steiner's celebrated *Times Literary Supplement* review essay on *Daphnia* and Carvill's work: "The secrecy of Carvill's text stems from no esoteric knowledge, from no abstruseness of underlying symbology. By themselves, the words are nakedly simple. Yet no earthly language, no common tongue, can rival this vehemence of vision and repose. It urges, realizes with visionary exactitude, the possibility that alternative languages, purer, more rigorous, flourish like coral growths at ever greater depths beneath the surface of language itself. Yet no more poignant paean to the body of the loved one, or the perishable brevity of her beauty and their love, exists in modern English."

Sophia took her Chromebook with that passage onscreen out to the balcony of her single studio in NYU's Washington Square Village graduate housing complex. There she could look down on the traffic and passers-by on Bleeker Street, where the young Melville had wandered, and feel the life flowing down the sidewalks, for New York is not America, but is America's window on the world. And through a window blows fresh air.

Sophia spent most of the fall semester fleshing out her insight into a proper dissertation topic. Every so often she checked her progress with Gaye, who always gave her the same warm, if cautious, endorsement. After majoring on writers like Robert Lowell and David Foster Wallace, whose struggles with their past reflected her own, Sophia hardly had to sidestep to focus on Carvill, but his work rather closed her off from other literature, confined her in the sound-worlds of those two sonnet cycles. She had been single since spring, with no relationship to distract her, which gave her more time and energy to concentrate on Carvill. She had her literature review essay ready before the eleventh week of her fall semester, just as the PhD guidelines required.

In front of the core dissertation committee, she felt a little less certain. She had her research question in mind right from the start, and finally framed it as a condensed version of her original remarks to Gaye. Dr. Kenyon, who had seen her through her doctoral exam, was staying on as her dissertation director, which helped calm her nerves. As it turned out, though, he was the only one to raise a genuine objection to her thesis.

"Do you feel you have enough personal affinity with Carvill to achieve real insight into his artistic personality and creative processes?" asked Dr. Amanda Green, who had coached her through her Critical Theory minor. She had a strong gender studies bias, and Sophia suspected she might have issues with her plan to get inside the head of such a masculine writer.

"I'm mostly looking at forensics rather than an imaginative sympathy, at least first off," she countered. "There's no full-length biography of Carvill published yet, and not so many personal memoirs of his life. There are still plenty of grey areas and unknowns in his past. I do believe I'd be breaking new ground."

Dr. Green pursed her lips, but leaned back in her chair and dropped that line of interrogation. None of the committee's other questions posed much of a challenge, and by the end, it was clear that the committee had accepted her essay and were ready to support her through the drafting of her actual dissertation proposal in the spring. Only Dr. Kenyon took her aside after his colleagues had gathered up their papers and left the book-lined faculty office, a frown creasing his dark features.

"I feel there's a fundamental ambiguity or disconnect at the core of your proposal, but I'm willing to accept that that stems from Carvill's work itself, and is something you'll address and resolve," he declared, staring her in the eyes. "And even if you never do, you'll produce some useful secondary literature on Carvill. But I'll be on the lookout for any signs that you're getting too wrapped up in this, especially if you start to overrun your time or funding. Save it for your own first book, that's my advice. It's for your own good. Trust me."

He squeezed her elbow before letting her go. Sophia was a little disconcerted: Dr. Kenyon had been a warm, even sympathetic supervisor, never one to warn her about her own plans. She spent the rest of the day wondering whether he had been cautioning her about something he saw in Carvill's work, or in herself.

⚬⚬

Winter break was one of the loneliest times of year for Sophia: other students were going home to their families, but she felt no pull to return to the folkish New England lanes of weatherboarded houses – those cold, snowbound parcels of indifference and neglect. Gaye was off to her own folks on the West Coast, and after her essay review, Sophia had no time or money left to plan any trips. Instead, she hung out in South Manhattan bars, retracing some of Carvill's wanderings in Village Bohemia. One lonely evening just after Christmas, she pulled on her Ralph Lauren parka and trudged out through the snow to the White Lady Tavern, one of Carvill's storied haunts, to see what she could find. Leonard the bartender had been working behind its celebrated marble bar for decades, and, it being a slow night, he stood her a lemon twist martini as he regaled her with his Carvill anecdotes. Leonard, it turned out, had known Carvill back in the 1990s, and felt quite some affinity for the fellow West Sider.

"You shouldn't get the wrong impression from his work," he confided, brushing his walrus whiskers. "Carvill was a very physical guy. Worked out at the gym, got into fights; he could be an ugly customer in a barroom brawl. That was the Irish in him, I suppose. Well read, yes: he always had a paperback stuck in his back pocket. But he looked a man who worked with his hands. If I hadda guess how he was going to make his mark, I'd 'a said as a sculptor or a stonemason, not a poet."

Sophia nodded and sipped her martini, hunched on her barstool. Leonard eyed her sympathetically.

"You sure you don't prefer a nip of whisky or a rum toddy, girl?" he asked her. "Martini's a cold drink for the snow."

"I'm fine with this, thanks," she replied, actually enjoying the chill zest of the gin.

"Suit yourself, hon, but just don't catch cold," Leonard replied. For all his Greenwich Village kudos, he was obviously a considerate man, gifted with the human touch.

"You think he had an artist's eye as well?" she asked, giving him her most ingratiating smile.

Leonard looked away for a moment. Then he reached down behind the bar, pulled open a drawer with a brass handle, and took out a single sheet of brown paper. Laying it down on the marble in front of her, he smoothed the creases in the sheet of thick brown packing roll.

"That's a sketch he did here in this bar, sitting in that booth over there," he remarked, pointing with his left thumb at a corner table. "He was gonna give it me as a free gift, but I stood him a drink for that. I've been planning to frame it, but there's so many other pictures on the back wall, it's hard to know where to hang it."

The sketch was a bravura portrait of Leonard, executed in chalk, highlights and shadows beautifully suggested by the gradations of brown and white. "He did that with the chalk off of the blackboard," Leonard mused. "See, there's his 'DC' signature in the corner. Some guy."

"Could I photograph this?" she asked, eyes on the makeshift canvas.

Leonard scrutinized her for a moment, then slowly nodded. "Just don't spread it around too widely, you hear? This is mine, and I aim to keep it." And after she had snapped the portrait with her phone, he carefully slipped it away.

***

By January, when Gaye and her other friends started to trickle back, Sophia had the germs of her dissertation proposal together, ready to enrol in Dissertation Seminar II for the formal drafting. Her preliminary hypothesis wasn't going to be any problem – she had all that down and ready to go. Sophia tended to work in binges of activity interspersed with long dry spells, rather correlated with her episodes of depression, and she decided to use the time on her hands before the proposal due date in late March to do some initial research. A first email exchange with the Bridwell

Art Library in Louisville in Kentucky highlighted Booklyn as the most likely starting point to trace Carvill's time in the art book scene. She decided to pay a visit in person, rather than use email or phone, and took the J train across the Williamsburg Bridge to Brooklyn. After a walk down Greenpoint Avenue to Booklyn, with the East River just in view beyond the WNYC Transmitter Park, she sat down with Carmen Noriega, the acting curator, and sipped Rainforest Alliance Certified tea as the homely, middle-aged vegan reminisced about Carvill.

"We ain't got too much time for day-trippers," Noriega sniffed. "There are plenty of authors and artists around who are ready to get behind a bigger run of copies, or get more involved in the bookmaking process. Carvill, yes, of course we heard the rumors: who hasn't? But we have our hands full with those who are genuinely committed, never mind those who parachute into the scene then just leave."

She sniffed again.

"Actually, it's the rumors I'm interested in," Sophia countered. "I'm trying to find out what Carvill did in the way of art books, and where. You know he's supposed to have produced two originals that no one has ever seen. At least, no one I've been able to find. But the rumors have to have started somewhere. Right now, it's more like, somebody knew somebody, who heard from somebody, that they had seen one of Desmond Carvill's art books."

Noriega pursed her lips. "Well, you could try Small Editions. Yes, I heard those rumors too. And they seemed to center around Small Editions. They're a good house. If Carvill wanted quality, he'd go there, for sure."

"Could you give me a name?" Sophia hazarded.

Noriega stopped, and eyed her a moment. "Thomas Reynolds. Talk to Thomas Reynolds at Small Editions. But don't say I sent you. There are enough Carvill stories floating around as it is. You can just say you overheard it at an art book show."

Sophia thanked her. "So where are they? I mean, of course I can Google it, but just so I know."

"They're down in Red Hook. Near Carroll Street, other end of the G train. Not the nicest neighborhood, but, well, they've been there for years without any trouble. Take care, though."

"I will, thank you." Sophia left Carmen Noriega to her tea, and decided not to chance the ride into Red Hook that day. On the way home, swiping through the Carvill photo archive on her phone, she paused at one of the more famous portraits of the poet, taken just prior to the publication of *Daphnia*; black and white, with Carvill gazing left of shot past the lens, cigarette poised in one hand, wisps of smoke mingling with his crisp locks. And she looked down at the text along the bottom edge of the picture: "Mark Fuller Photography."

She decided to talk with Gaye about that, and went round to her friend's room as soon as she got home. Gaye turned off her usual clangor of black metal and hunkered down to examine the photo.

"So what is it you've got to show to me?" she asked, glancing up brightly. "Yea, I know that shot; seen it on a dozen back covers. What about it?"

"That was taken by Mark Fuller," Sophia pointed out, chewing her thumb. "And Carvill got himself snapped by many of the other big names of that era: Masayoshi Sukita, Brooks Kraft, Gene Shaw. All just before his first volume appeared."

"So?"

Sophia lowered her thumb and folded her arms. "Well, all the evidence suggests that Carvill was hungry for fame prior to his first book's appearance; desperate for it. Currying favor with all the leading lights in the New York scene, getting his photo taken with them, hitting up all the legendary places, hustling for exposure. Then, when it all comes together, when the fame he courted finally arrives, he drops out of sight. What's up with that?"

Gaye shrugged. "The light dawned, maybe? He saw sense?"

"I think it's more personal than that. I think it has something to do with his first muse, the girl he wrote *Daphnia* about, whoever she was. The published literature links *Daphnia* to at least three actual girlfriends of Carvill, and only one of them has actually spoken out about her time with him. The others have gone off the grid. So, follow me here: critics link the Daphnia of Carvill's sonnets, as well as the water flea, with Daphne the classical naiad, who Apollo chases into the reeds, where she turns into a laurel. And after her transformation, Daphne becomes the crown of poets laureate, the laurel wreath. So, some critics believe that Carvill canonized his first love as the spirit of lyric poetry, as a thank-you for the inspiration that made him a major poet. Maybe once he had his masterpiece, and his muse, that was enough for him, and he didn't need the validation anymore."

"Well, don't forget that he came out with another collection about a completely different woman just a few years after the first," Gaye pointed out. "He must have been hungry for fresh inspiration, if you're right, and sniffing around in the shadows."

"True," Sophia conceded. "But whatever went down, the original Daphnia has never re-emerged, so if she was dumped for his Nyx, no one ever heard about it."

"So you think he has a ménage à trois going on, wherever it is he's run away to?" Gaye chuckled acidly. "A swamp cabin in the Everglades? A ski lodge in Colorado? Canada, even? Europe?"

"I don't know. But if he does have a threesome going, that'd be one reason to keep out of sight. I mean, imagine the gossip columns, the paparazzi. America's greatest love poet and his love nest."

"Yeah, maybe if he wanted the spotlight, he should have kept his dick inside his pants." Gaye's grin broadened. "Men, eh?"

"Well, I think I know who I'm going to ask about it," Sophia said, half to herself, looking down at the photograph.

In complete contrast to Carvill, Mark Fuller was not exactly hard to run down: she found the legendary fashion photographer perched on a stool in his favorite East Village cafe, nervous fingers fumbling with a rolled-up cigarette, his sleek state-of-the-art Macbook Air stained a bizarre bronze patina by nicotine.

"Yeah, Carvill wanted the limelight back then," he concurred, after Sophia had introduced herself. "Always looking for ways to get into the frame. Not that the guy was a fake or anything; even back in the day, you could see he had the talent. For what, though: that wasn't so clear. Me, I figured him for an up-and-coming performance artist on the make. I was going through a kinetic period, you know, figures in motion, so he fitted right in with where I was at the time."

"I was thinking the girl who inspired *Daphnia* might have drawn him away from that," Sophie suggested.

Fuller nodded sharply, like a wary heron checking its six before its next dart at the fish. "Might have been. He was seriously into his squeeze: Dana Novak. I'd see them all the time at parties together. She was a BFA dance student at Fordham University: slight, a dancer's figure, always wore her hair done up in a bun on top of her head, you know, like dancers do. Had some Central European blood in her too: dark eyes and high cheekbones. Not sure she ever made it past ensemble dancer, though. Matter of fact, I'm not sure what became of her at all. She dropped out of sight around the same time Carvill did."

Sophia remembered that name, one of Carvill's girlfriends listed in the secondary literature as a potential model for *Daphnia*. "You never photographed her? Or took them together?"

Fuller shook his head. "I had plenty of dancers to photograph in those days. Slavic types too. That was then. These days I prefer American beauty. Like yours." And his brown fingernails brushed her cheekbone.

Back in her NYU room, Sophie examined herself in the bathroom mirror: gamine figure, amber blonde locks whose highlights shone out naturally after soaking up summer sun, wide forehead, big green eyes, generous mouth. And the subtle, insidious voices started niggling once again at the back of her mind: look how bland and insipid you are, so characterless, so cliched, so diluted honey-sweet, so plain, so flat, so dull, so worthless. You would never ever stand out in a crowd, let alone interest a man like Mark Fuller – or Desmond Carvill. Your work is pointless, your struggles are futile; why not just go find yourself an unfaithful banker husband, have a litter of kids out in the burbs, and maybe make a little extra pocket money on the side from insurance commercials or shampoo ads. Your qualifications will wow hubby and the neighbors with your refinement and polish, because let's face it, your insights are superficial, and your mind second-rate. Just give it up.

⚬⚬⚬

The depressive episode that followed occupied much of Sophia's time before the submission of her dissertation proposal, but come March, she had most of the structure down, and had gathered enough resolve to take a trip out to Small Editions. Carmen Noriega's version of "near" turned out to be almost a mile from the G train to the fringes of the Red Hook Container Terminal, through parts of Brooklyn she'd rather not see again, and she decided to call Uber once her visit was done, or catch the Pier 6 ferry across to Governors Island. At the end of her walk, though, she found a castellated red-brick building with a green awning over its porch, a small reassuring fortress of culture in the bleak warehouse district.

Thomas Reynolds, pale and skeletal, with the creased face and tattered black cottons of an aging Goth, ushered her past the gallery space and upstairs to his office. What he had to tell her that he didn't want the rest of the workshop to hear, she had no idea, but his little performance did intrigue her. She noticed that he didn't introduce her to any of the other craftspeople, and apparently hadn't shared her email appointment with the girl on the front desk. Reynolds knew exactly what she was there for from her email, though, and got straight down to business.

"We often create custom binding structures to reflect a book's content," he explained, miming the process with his slender hands as he talked. "Carvill was a special case. He presented us with exactly fourteen sheets of vellum, no more or less, already inscribed. He wanted those bound appropriately: enshrined, he said. They were the autograph pages of *Nyx*, his manuscript, executed in perfect freehand, without a single flaw in the calligraphy."

"Vellum?" Sophia asked, distracted by the lovely panorama of the Manhattan skyline across the East River beyond his office windows.

"Vellum," he nodded. "Preserved and treated calfhide. There's a modern synthetic variety, made from cotton, but the echt vellum is from a young calf, and the finest grades are from the skin of an unborn one."

"People still do that?" she wondered, suddenly fully focused.

"The Brits still print their Acts of Parliament on vellum. Some diplomas are still written on vellum. Scrolls of the Torah are made from vellum." Reynolds extended the wave of his hand to encompass the workshop outside his office walls. "People think of a library or a bookstore as a cemetery of dead trees, but they're every bit as much a graveyard of dead animals. All those leather covers, tanned parchments and ivory bindings; or the bonefolder, our tool of the trade. Even that name tells you a lot..." He gazed at his shelves, as though mentally cataloging his own tools.

"But why would Carvill do that?"

"I don't know: he never told me." Reynolds shrugged. "Maybe he was in love with the feel of it; he wouldn't have been the first artist to fetishize his medium. Maybe it was something to do with word symbolism; vellum shares a common root with a whole cluster of other words that would interest a poet like Carvill – velar consonant, veil, et cetera. Or maybe he just wanted to make sure his penmanship was preserved: vellum can last for over a thousand years, far more durable than paper."

Reynolds leaned closer and lowered his voice. "All that's speculation, but I will tell you one thing: I don't know what tanning or coloring process he used, but the vellum was dark. Beautiful quality, thin, fine, delicate, but dark. A weird shade, hard to describe. Somehow he'd made his darker red script stand out against it, but the overall effect was almost occult, like some sorcerer's grimoire."

Despite herself, for no clear reason, Sophia shuddered and caught her breath as her imagination threw up those pages in her mind's eye.

"So what about this calligraphy?" she pressed. "Was it really that special? Everyone knows Carvill produced his sonnet cycles in two original art books, but could those sheets have been the actual manuscript?"

Reynolds looked defensive for a moment. "Like I say, he didn't tell me anything. He just told our craftworkers what he needed doing, and we did it. I tell you, though, if that was his original manuscript, I can see why he placed so much value on it. We could have given him the best, most artistic layout and typesetting you'd ever be able to find anywhere, stuff that would take your breath away. Letterpress and intaglio, we can do it all. On papyrus fit for the pharaohs. But Carvill, he wanted only his own pages preserved, his own penmanship. If he used a pen. He wanted them bound; not mounted like bookplates, but sewn into a proper leather binding. He was very specific. He asked for Levant Morocco binding, goatskin, tanned with traditional techniques, and dyed a dark blood red with equally traditional pigments. And he wanted cedarwood boards, cedar of Lebanon; Biblical, he said."

"So how did his actual script look?"

Reynolds looked more than a little dazed, as he slowly recounted what he had seen.

"Unbelievable. I had a chance to examine the sheets up close, you know; held them in my hands as we were sewing them into the binding. On a typical antique vellum leaf, from an medieval illuminated manuscript, you'll see prick marks in the sheet, for ruling lines as writing guides. But there were none on Carvill's pages, and yet the lines of the poetry were perfectly straight. And I saw him tool the title and the design himself onto the cover. Her name, Nyx, and a full moon. A blood moon, he called it. Normally you trace a gilding design onto the leather, and then tool it before gilding. Carvill didn't. He drew the designs, then tooled them with a swivel knife, himself. Not a single hesitation or second thought. They were perfect."

They both fell silent for a moment. Finally, Sophia stuttered into hesitant speech.

"No, we didn't take any pictures or photocopies," Reynolds had already guessed her question. "He wouldn't allow it. He brought us the vellum sheets, told us what he wanted, took the finished book, paid in cash, and left. But look, if you want to get sight of his manuscripts, try talking to his agent or his publishers. I saw how fixated Carvill was on his writing; he would have been just as focused when it came to typesetting and proofreading. My money would be on a really intensive, concentrated layout process with the publishers of the first print editions, with a lot of cross-checking and comparison. Go talk to them."

April filled Sophia's days with a cruelly punishing schedule of drafting, rewriting and laborious editing to lick her dissertation proposal into shape. She worried at it relentlessly, redrafting again and again, until finally she was as satisfied as she could be with the twelve pages on which her future depended. Once the proposal was submitted, she had a couple of weeks in hand before her proposal defense before the committee, and she decided to use the time to talk to Carvill's publishers.

First to bite was St. Mark's Press, *Daphnia*'s publisher, domiciled in the Flatiron Building. Gene Bachmann, former poetry editor at St. Mark's and now head of fiction commissioning, occupied a point office in the Flatiron, overlooking Madison Square Park and north to the Empire State. Bachmann ought to be at the pinnacle of literary power and influence, at the heart of the world's publishing capital, yet Sophia found him hunkered in his cheese-wedge suite like a fugitive.

"Grace Weather, his agent, brought the book to us," he explained. "I guess you know that already, right? Everybody does. Even then, her rep was strong enough to get me to look at anything she wanted to show to me. And when she read me the first sonnet, I was sold: I knew we had to have the book. But when she started reeling off Carvill's conditions, that's when things began to get weird."

"How so?" Sophia raised an eyebrow, legs crossed in her most professional skirt.

"We worked from photographs. Not photocopies or scans, you understand: photos. They were given to us on a single memory card, a CompactFlash card back in those days. Weather watched us the entire time, to make sure that no one copied the PNGs. We transcribed what was on the screen, triple-checked it against the images, then she took the memory card and left."

"Do you remember anything special about how the text looked?"

He paused. "It was odd. Handwritten in neat cursive strokes, beautiful flawless calligraphy, but the lines were ever so slightly blurry at the edges. And it was dark red. Like something out of *Lord of the Rings*."

"It's not the first time I've heard that," Sophia admitted, winning a half surprised, half respectful glance from Bachmann. "Do you have any idea why it was like that?"

Bachmann shrugged. "Not a clue. I never got to meet Carvill; he never came to any of the launch events and readings, never participated in the publicity and marketing process at all. But if that really was his handwriting, in his own manuscript, he could have had a fine career as a calligrapher, if he hadn't been a great poet. They were perfect."

"You wouldn't have any lead to the agent, would you?" she probed.

"You've done your homework on her as well, I'm sure. She's almost as reclusive as he is. Correspondence goes to a P.O. box, royalties get paid into a corporate account, awards and honorary fellowships are accepted on her behalf by third parties. She's hardly ever seen in public. Carvill's like a black hole: people around him get sucked behind an event horizon into some parallel universe." He shivered. "After working on him, I just couldn't do poetry anymore."

Sophia sent a letter to Grace Weather's P.O. box anyway, not really expecting a response. When they sat down together in the spring sunshine on the benches at the east end of the Washington Square Village complex, watching the sparrows bathe and play in the little spiral fountain on Mercer Street, Gaye was pessimistic about her chances of further progress.

"I think you've done enough primary research, girl," she affirmed. "Those art books are a blind alley. Save it for when you're a Doctor, a made woman, on a tenure track with nice fat research grants. Then you'll have all the time in the world to do your Lara Croft thing and run them down."

"Now you're sounding like my dissertation director," Sophia sniffed. "So you think I should just let it drop? But I feel like I've been getting so close, you know?"

"Yeah, where others have been before, and gotten nowhere. You've said as much yourself before now."

"No, scholars have been looking for Carvill himself, or secrets in his past to enable them to better comprehend the verse; not the books themselves," Sophia corrected her. "To be able to follow his original penstrokes, the rhythm, the hesitations, the assertions – that could unlock so much."

"So like I say, save it." Gaye folded Sophia's hand between hers and looked her in the eye, smiling wanly. Something about her expression, the hesitancy and trace of wistfulness, made Sophia pause and examine her friend again.

"There's something up with you, isn't there?" she asked.

Gaye nodded and looked down. "I think I'm in love," she admitted. "And it feels like the real thing this time."

"Hey, girl," Sophia grinned, rubbing Gaye's shoulder with her free hand. 'You didn't tell me anything. Who's the lucky fella?"

"Well, you've been too busy with your research," Gaye sniffed. "He's from the Stern School. He complimented me on my tattoo, and we got talking, and well, one thing led to another…"

"Wow, you minx," Sophia breathed. "So come on, tell me all about him…"

The ensuing girl talk didn't entirely drive Gaye's remarks from her mind. Had she been getting too wrapped up in Carvill, too drawn to the flame? Others thought so too, apparently. When Sophia defended her dissertation proposal before the committee in early May, the defense itself went relatively well; the committee's queries were few and relatively perfunctory. Around the issue of summer funding for required research, though, things got sticky.

"We feel you've done enough at this point to warrant continuing," Dr. Kenyon said, knitting his knuckles together on the table in front of him. "Your proposal is firm. Further field investigation, let alone a search for these rumored books, would be a waste of your time and the faculty's money." And he brushed her objections aside.

Sophia had no choice but to concede the committee's decision. But Dr. Kenyon was just as recalcitrant when she buttonholed him after the session broke up.

"I think you're getting too close to this," he insisted. "You have original insights and I'm impressed by your scholarship; don't blow it all on a wild goose chase after some artefacts that may no longer exist."

"But I've had multiple eye-witness accounts," she pleaded. "They're out there, I know it. With them in front of me, I know I could really get inside his head, see things in the words that no one else has seen."

"Sophia, heed my advice and take a step back," he cautioned her, putting a hand on her wrist. "I've seen this happen before. Don't get lost in the sonnets. They're a hall of mirrors. Some readers get drawn into them and never come out. I don't need to tell you that some critics equate Carvill with poets who wrote their work while actually clinically insane, channeling madness – late Hölderlin, Georg Trakl, Gerard de Nerval. Remember that graduate researcher from Texas? The one they say is institutionalized now after studying Carvill too hard? If you try to force yourself into Carvill's mindset when he wrote those sonnets, it'll be your mind that breaks. Language was never meant to do what his poems do. They're a beautifully baited trap."

Sophia remembered the story. "I thought she was another myth. You think I should go down there? Interview her?"

Dr. Kenyon gave her a cool, straight look. "That's what I mean," he said quietly.

That night, Sophia had a nightmare. In the dream, she was groping through black and red catacombs pulsing to the rhythm of one of Gaye's black metal tracks, towards a dark chamber where fourteen birdcages hung, each with fourteen bars, each cage a Carvill sonnet, each bar a line, only the cages were the actual wiry little ribcages of the singing birds, every bird its own cage, and she knew somewhere in the depths of her dream awareness that the chamber was the right ventricle of Carvill's beating heart.

After that dream, Sophia might have heeded Dr. Kenyon's warning, if not for the call she received out of the blue a few days later from a blocked caller ID. A woman's voice, mature, measured, unfamiliar, asked her to confirm who she was.

"Grace Weather here," the voice went on. "You do know who I am, I'm sure." And then the woman asked her to name an evening in the next few days when she would be free.

"My driver will pick you up, on the corner of Bleeker Street and Bowery," Grace Weather finished, then rang off without further explanation. Sophia looked disbelievingly at her phone display, wondering for a moment if it could be a prank call, but then what prankster would know about her research and the reports she had already unearthed about Grace Weather?

Prior to the meeting, Sophia bought a pocket voice recorder from the Best Buy on Broadway, determined to record whatever Grace Weather had to say, with or without permission. What had led her to follow

Carvill into seclusion, Sophia pondered, as she walked back down East Houston afterwards, the late afternoon sunshine which reflected off window glass further down the street half blinding her. But then, this was New York, with everyone in their own head space doing all kinds of private things, she thought, watching a crazed dirt biker in a German army helmet wheelie down the street, yelling, spinning, and doing burnouts at each red light.

A luxurious town car with tinted rear windows pulled up at the kerb on Bleeker Street and Bowery at the designated time. The driver slid down his side window to ask her name, then let her in. Clearly they were headed somewhere on the Upper West Side, though by the time they reached their destination, the sun had already set and the streets were dark. The driver stopped outside a large, anonymous, Art Deco apartment building, with a name but no street number that she could discern, gave her a room number and a door code for the front entrance, and she buzzed herself in.

Sophia found herself remembering *The Shining*, and any number of other Stephen King ghost stories, as she stepped out of the elevator into a corridor of identical, beautifully detailed doors, and she felt like a psychic investigator as she switched on the voice recorder in her jacket pocket before stepping up to the security peephole to knock. Grace Weather, when she opened the door, looked just like her photographs, though in the dim lamplight inside the luxurious suite it was hard to tell how much she had aged, how much more gray there was at her temples, how many more lines were etched around her eyes. Grace Weather seated herself behind a huge desk that gave the front room the air of an office, despite the TV and three-piece lounge suite, leaned back in her swivel chair, and took a moment to examine Sophia before she began.

"Help yourself to the water there." She pointed at a row of glasses and bottled mineral water on her lacquer desk set. "I'll explain why I brought you here like this. You see, as custodian of the Carvill estate, naturally I keep an eye on research into Mister Carvill's work, and stay in touch with his publishers and former associates. Mister Carvill left instructions that if anyone researching his work and personal history showed enough insight and understanding, I should extend the opportunity of a personal meeting. You have met the criteria."

Grace Weather waited for that to sink in, then continued.

"I should warn you that the conditions are onerous. I need you to examine them in writing, and if you decide to accept them, sign an agreement here and now. If you do so, at a future date a driver will take you to a secret location to meet with him, for a set period of time, probably around a fortnight. Afterwards, you will still be bound by the terms of the agreement, which will apply indefinitely."

She slipped a manilla folder across the baize surface of the desk to Sophia. Leafing through the document inside, Sophia read carefully until the third page, then stopped, with a sudden twist in her gut.

"You're asking me to pay $5 million for any use of information I obtain from a meeting with Desmond Carvill, in any medium?" she asked.

Grave Weather shook her head. "Read on," she urged. "The agreement doesn't require you to pay that amount, it simply gives the estate the option to grant a fee waiver, so long as what you publish is preauthorized by us. If you publish without authorization, you are liable for the full fee."

"But I never could afford that," Sophia replied, then her voice trailed off as the significance of the arrangement dawned on her.

"That's the point," the older woman confirmed. "This is more enforceable than an NDA. And Mister Carvill's estate will interpret a public admission that you met him, or even disclosure of the text of this agreement, as an unauthorized use of information. The courts would deem that you derived personal and material benefit from the publicity, and would rule accordingly. Given his mystique, you know that that would stick. I assure you, though, that this only applies in case of unauthorized disclosure. And you can always refuse to sign."

"And what if I refuse, then walk away and tell the world that I was made a crazy extortionate offer to meet Desmond Carvill?" Sophia shot back, angry despite herself.

"Then Mister Carvill's publishers, and anyone else associated with his estate, will receive instructions to refuse cooperation with you," Grace Weather replied, tone calm and placatory, despite her words. "For your current project and for any future research. We only want to protect his interests, and to forestall any more rumors. There are enough of those already. But if you do agree to sign, you can have access that no one else has. A full two weeks with the poet himself, open dialog. And we really would allow you to use authorized material, with a full fee waiver. The agreement states that, and you have my word."

"It still seems insanely heavy."

"No one wants another Harper Lee situation, you understand," Grace Weather sighed. "And Mister Carvill is a recluse, who values his privacy. He wants to protect it."

"Can I take this away, get an opinion, and think about it?" Sophia replied, holding up the draft agreement by its corner staple between thumb and forefinger.

Grace Weather shook her head again. "This is a one-time offer. And that time is now. Please, take your time to study it. I'll leave you to make your decision."

She got up, smoothed down her perfect twin-set, and walked through to the adjoining room. Sophia heard her pouring something into an ice-filled glass, while she pored over the clauses on the stapled papers like a map of a minefield, alert for any loopholes, any hidden threats. Everything seemed exactly as Grace Weather had outlined. She had no idea if any court in New York would actually enforce it, but she could not see that she had any other choice.

"Umm, Miss Weather?" she asked, knocking on the door frame of Grace Weather's spotlessly white kitchen, where the agent stood gazing out of the window into the darkness. "I accept. Where do I sign?"

Grace Weather turned back to her and gave a small, half sad smile. "Here, let me take you through it," she said, and led Sophia back to the desk. She showed Sophia where to fill in her name and address, and what clauses to initial. Finally, they both signed and dated the last page.

"We'll be in touch to confirm the dates and where to meet," Grace Weather concluded, sliding Sophia's copy of the completed document back across the desk in a sealed envelope. "My driver will take you back and drop you wherever you need to go." Sophia gathered up her things and left the agent in her suite, still sipping her long drink.

Afterwards, she agonized over whether to tell Gaye, but her best friend saved her the trouble by disappearing for a sudden vacation with her new guy. She stuck the agreement out of the way in her bottom drawer and erased the recording too, afraid what prosecution might ensue if it ever came to light.

⁓

When the call finally came, Sophia had her Moleskine notebook and pen all ready to jot down the details. It was easy enough to recuse herself from hall for a fortnight's break, and she primed her NYU account and voicemail with the same explanation.

Grace Weather had designated a deserted parking lot in East Harlem, near an on-ramp for FDR Drive. Sophia wondered about taking her case filled with everything for a fortnight, but finally decided on the bare minimum, and stuffed her rucksack like a vacationing backpacker. Despite her light summer jacket and the June heat, she shivered a little as she stood waiting in the empty lot a few mornings later, just within sight of the East River. No other cars were within a hundred yards of her; nor, she realized, were any security cameras.

About fifteen minutes after the appointed time, an unmarked white van turned into the lot and pulled up beside her. It was the only vehicle she had seen enter the place. A solid-looking individual in a leather jacket jumped out and strode over to her.

"Miss Amory?" he asked. "Grace Weather asked me to pick you up."

Without further introduction, he slid open the van's side door and held out his hand for her backpack. "You'll have to stay in the rear for the journey," he explained half apologetically, with a classier accent than she'd expected from his looks. He took her heavy rucksack from her with one hand, dropped it gently into the back of the van as though it weighed nothing, and turned back to her.

"Empty your pockets and the contents of your purse, please."

She did as she was asked, spilling the innards of her imitation Birkin bag onto the van's metal floor. Once everything was out, she turned to him defiantly. He looked her up and down with cool appraisal.

"Sorry, Ma'am, but I'm going to have to do a pat-down. Please stand with your arms away from your sides."

She bit back a retort, on the verge of calling the whole thing off. But finally she stood passive, arms akimbo, as he slid his big hands over her limbs and body without a trace of sensuality.

"There," he concluded, stepping away and nodding. Then he picked her phone out of the small pile of gear in the back of the van, and passed it to her.

"Remove the battery and the SIM card, please. It'll be returned to you at the end of your visit."

She teased the phone's case open with her fingernail, pulled out battery and card, then handed everything to him.

"Thank you," he said, and pocketed them, then helped her gently into the van. Inside, there was a single jump seat bolted to one wall, with a seat belt and a grab strap. The driver took a bottle of water from his own seat and passed it to her.

"We'll be a while, I'm afraid," he explained, and without further ado, slid the side door shut. Grace folded down the jump seat and strapped in, while he started the van. She had only a restricted view over the high front seat, and the windows in the van's rear doors were taped over. Around her were some Amazon boxes, crates and cartons, and a couple of plastic carboys of chemicals, securely strapped down. The van pulled out, swung onto the road, and juddered between intersections and crossings for a few minutes before turning onto what must be FDR Drive.

Traffic noise around her smoothed to a steady hiss. From the way the van swung right, and the hollow metallic rumble under its wheels, she guessed they were crossing the Willis Avenue Bridge, headed north into the Bronx and onto Interstate 87, meaning they must be ascending the valley of the Hudson, towards Germantown, Albany and the wilderness areas beyond Saratoga Springs. Carvill could be anywhere up there, hiding out in the Adirondacks. The driver turned on the van's music deck. David Bowie's "Joe the Lion" segued into "Heroes," as the light reflecting in through the windshield turned greener. Sophia tried to pass the time by going over some notes in her Moleskine binder, but the monotony of the journey and the featureless interior of the van were mesmerizing, and she found herself drifting off to sleep with her cheek resting against the seat belt. An uncertain number of hours later, she was jolted awake as the van slowed and turned, leaving the expressway. With no phone screen and no wristwatch, she had lost track of time ages ago, though an ache in her bladder told her at least a few hours must have passed. All the same, she took a gulp of water from the plastic bottle and looked around her, trying once more to peer over the top of the front seats. That told her nothing more than that they were driving through woods now, with only occasional breaks in the forest cover on both sides. The sunlight looked somehow thinner, and the air felt colder.

When the driver finally stopped the van and killed the engine, the first thing that struck her was the quiet: so pervasive that every sound, from his feet on the earth to the side door sliding open, seemed individually shrink-wrapped in its coating of silence. She stepped out of the van into a clearing surrounded by mature forest growth, with no obvious breaks in any direction. Even the road out of the clearing was a gravelled earth track, soon lost among the trees. "Here you are, Ma'am," the driver explained, then went around to the back of the van to start unloading. She stood on the yielding earth and looked around her: a one-storey log cabin filled the far end of the forest glade, with outbuildings sprawling on either side. She smelled timber, resins, leaves. A door swung open on the cabin verandah, and a denim-jacketed figure stepped out and came down the steps to meet her.

Desmond Carvill had changed in the decade or so since his last pictures, in more than the lines in his face and the salt-and-pepper grizzling in his hair. Those early photographs showed, without exception, a self-conscious figure, poised for the shot, wary of the camera. Now Carvill looked totally indifferent to any watching eye, at his ease, completely relaxed and spontaneous. He fixed Sophia with a green-eyed gaze and extended a hand.

"Sophia Amory? Desmond Carvill. Welcome, I'm pleased to have you here."

She took his hand, feeling the firm muscle behind his handshake, the exact, calculated pressure. He eyed her frankly, speculatively, as though pondering something. "John took care of you?" he asked. "He runs my errands and gets me things, but he's no chaffeur."

"He was fine," she answered. "But I do need to use your bathroom."

"There's an outhouse attached to the workshop over there." He jerked a thumb towards one of the outbuildings. She hurried away while Carvill helped John unload, swapping short, blunt remarks. As well as the bathroom, she needed a moment to recover her poise, and be fully in control of body and mind before facing Carvill again.

Once she was inside its wooden door, however, the workshop was such a distraction that she almost forgot her itching bladder. A workbench with carpenter's hand and power tools neatly laid out, and shelved around it, several animal skins stretched on frames hung on the walls, a few sketches and photographs mounted at eye level, one or two sculptures and objets d'art placed at random here and there; she could almost imagine herself transported back to Brancusi's studio. Carvill obviously was keeping up his craft-based skills: she almost wanted to start jotting down notes straight away.

The toilet was just an earth closet, with a roll of paper on a bent piece of wire and a tin sink, but the seat over the hole in the ground was beautifully planed and smoothed, with a lovely grain: she felt somehow that Carvill must have done it himself. There was no mirror above the sink for her to compose herself in, so she primped quickly in a vanity mirror from her purse before re-emerging. John took a last half-smiling glance at her, flicked her a casual salute as he jumped back into the driver's seat, then backed the van out of the clearing and drove off. The engine noise receded down the forest road, and she was alone with Carvill.

"Come on in: I'll show you your room," he invited her, hefting her rucksack on his shoulder. He spoke with a distinct brogue, his Irish ancestry as evident in his voice as in his looks. More solidly built than she had expected as well, she thought, looking up at his shoulders as he led her inside.

The front door opened into a wide timbered main room, with sofas along both sides and a long wooden dining table dividing it from the kitchen area along the rear wall. Carvill stuck out his right hand and opened a door in the far corner to reveal a large square book-lined room with a double bed covered in an Indian blanket. "This is the guest bedroom," he explained, dumping her pack on the bed. "Do you need to take a bit to unpack your stuff?"

"Um, I guess," she responded, suddenly unsure what to say or do.

"Just come and find me when you're done: I'll be around," he finished, and left her alone in the room.

Looking around, Sophia realized that she had been half expecting to find Daphnia, or Nyx, or any number of other Muses, waiting for her at Carvill's place beside the poet himself, in the same kind of ménage that she had joked about with Gaye. Or if not the girls themselves, traces of their presence.

She kept looking for those traces as she pulled her clothes out of her backpack and stowed them away neatly in the drawers and cupboards of the clean, bare room, but found nothing – even the interiors of the cabinets seemed to have been swept. But she realized something else as she unpacked her stuff: the drawers and cupboard doors were all formed from boards of through-sawn wood, mostly with the curve of the trunk still in the board. The effect was the same as the main room, that the whole cabin was a seamless organic whole.

Once she was unpacked, Carvill whipped up a filling supper of ham and eggs fried on an iron skillet: like many artists and craftspeople she had known, he was a good short-order cook. "The place is beautifully clean and well-kept," she remarked over her plate as they sat together at the dining table, munching their meal and sipping chilled microbrewed beers from the fridge, with ambient music playing quietly in the background.

"Oh, there's an old woman from a few cabins down who comes in to clean for me every week. She keeps some fine laying hens too," he replied, stirring his mess of eggs with the prongs of his fork. "John helps out at times, of course."

"I'd sort of expected that you… wouldn't be alone?" she hinted.

"Oh, you mean the girls?" he chuckled. "Well, they're no longer with me, though they're still very much here in spirit. Things change, and we all move on."

She raised an eyebrow at that. Carvill leaned back in his wooden chair, legs hooked under the table, a mouthful of ham speared on the end of his fork.

"I expect you'll be wanting to take some time to talk about my work," he began, through a mouthful of food. "Well, ye'd better know I don't have much of a schedule. I get up early and take walks in the forest before breakfast, but after that, it's not much but reading, and writing, and working on the house. Ye won't mind if I leave it all up to the mood of the moment: I'll either be in the study, or just follow the sound of tools. Oh, and anything you see here that you need, or want to use, take it, but don't break it."

They both chuckled briefly. "Internet?" she hazarded softly. "Phone?"

Carvill sobered. "I'm sorry, girl," he sighed. "Ye must understand why I can't allow that. And even if I could, there's no phone reception here up among the mountains. A carrier pigeon couldn't find us here."

"Mister Carvill, you have me at a disadvantage," she quipped primly, and the mood softened again. She had expected him somehow to be intimidating, she had expected herself to be as breathy and tongue-tied as any starstruck teenager, but somehow the warmth and intimacy of the house and Carvill's manner relaxed her, put her at her ease, encouraged her to stretch out and open up. She found herself talking about herself, rather than asking all the questions that had been pressing at the back of her mind all through her journey.

Carvill finally pushed his chair back from the table and stood up. "You're starting to flag," he pointed out, not unkindly. "I know it doesn't feel like you should be tired, but the long journey coupled with the clear mountain air up here does that to people. Take a shower or a bath before bed if you like, or do it first thing in the morning, it's all one to me. Trust me, you'll sleep like the dead. There's fresh towels in your room. I'll sit up a bit and do some work before turning in."

He helped her to her feet with his firm hand on her shoulder, proving his diagnosis right. The bathroom, opening off the main room beside the kitchen area, proved too tempting to resist, with its big jacuzzi-style tub, and she ran a hot bath before bed, glad to find that there was no problem with the hot water system, no matter how isolated Carvill was. "Zero net energy with bi-directional photovoltaics, and backup batteries for whenever the grid goes down, which happens about once every two months up here," he explained.

When she crossed to the bathroom in the thick woollen gown he had left hanging on the back of her door, she saw Carvill at his desk in the front study, tapping away at the biggest laptop she had ever seen. After her luxurious bath, lying between clean cotton sheets in her pyjamas, surrounded by the smell of pinewood and the soft sighing of the wind in the trees outside, she felt like a child again, back in summer camp, and fell immediately into a deep, restful sleep.

***

Carvill repeated his kitchen performance for her first breakfast with him, and Sophia went with the flow, buoyed up by the sense of detached unreality; Carvill the legend, now cooking her breakfast, had ushered her into the realm of myth. Every moment she spent there, she knew, could be parlayed into decades at the apex of her profession; she didn't even need to make an effort to succeed. The fortunate child favored of the fairies, she reflected, in one of her few time-outs from concentration on Carvill.

He proved surprisingly adept at answering questions while giving away relatively little, parrying adroitly, deferring detailed responses. Secrecy clearly hadn't stopped at the borders of his property. One confusing thing she realised was that she was no longer so concerned with the battery of questions she had lined up about his life and past work, as with what he was working on now. Carvill looked pretty businesslike seated at his laptop, but she wondered if that was staged for her benefit. From what she knew and guessed of Carvill's writing methods, that was the complete opposite of how he would set about creating new poetry, and occasional journalism really did not seem his style. Which begged the question: what was he really doing up here? Was this reclusive existence of craft work and household maintenance really enough for a man like Carvill?

Hunting he took seriously; that much was obvious. Sophia recognized all the signs from her New England childhood: the slender gun cabinet unobtrusively bolted to the wall just inside the front door, with three rifles locked away, including a beautiful Sako Finnlight; a vest full of pockets and his camo jacket hung on the coat hooks; the antlers mounted on the cabin beams, with plaques dating from the last few years. Luckily they were out of the hunting season: she didn't relish the prospect of Carvill bringing home his quarry and dressing a buck carcass in the front yard. But even now, he was apparently devoted to his summer game scouting, and liked to walk the deer trails with a scope and sachets of deer minerals, to keep an eye on the hardwood pockets. Carvill the New Yorker, the Manhattanite, had become a woodsman.

"Alright, I guessed you'd ask," he admitted, when she pressed him on it. "I need the hides. You saw some in the studio already. Naturally, I got into the habit once I moved up here. I make my own vellum, you see. I could buy the stuff and get John to ship it up to me from New York, but I prefer it this way: like an architect, you know? Using local materials? Here, let me show you."

He led her out to the workshed that she had looked around when she first arrived, and left the door open so the stuffy interior could air out in the warm early summer morning, then took one of the smaller stretching frames down off its hook, and laid it on the workbench.

"Swivel knife," he explained, picking a short tool with a cylindrical handle and an angled chisel-like blade from one rack. "Normally, I'd take the skin off the stretcher, but this one I think I can do freehand." He looked down at the stretched hide for a moment, composing himself. "A lot of it is in the posture and the breathing. You have to time the rhythm of your breathing to the work, and hold it during each stroke, then inhale and exhale in between, else you'll throw yourself off the line." He said nothing more, taking a final quiet breath, hesitated, then took the frame in his left hand, and executed a series of rapid twisting strokes with the right, his whole forearm weaving in and out. Sophia watched him, rapt.

"There," he said finally, releasing his breath, and held up the frame for her inspection. He had inscribed her first name, perfectly centered in the little canvas, with a bare minimum of curlicues and flourishes. Not an upstroke or a descender was out of place. "Sophia: Wisdom. Needs a bit of cleaning up, maybe, but here: it's for you."

He held it out to her. Sophia took the wooden frame, a lump in her throat.

"And in case you're wondering, that's how I did it," he added, a cooler, more detached appraisal in his gaze. She blushed.

Carvill might not even regard poetry as a conceptual process at all, she speculated afterwards, when she hung his gift up on an empty nail in her room. What she had witnessed was certainly more like a performance. That made her even less ready to frame her questions in words. She no longer felt any sense of urgency. With no phone, and no clocks or computer screens around the cabin, she was already losing track of time.

⚬

Carvill left on his hikes in the morning, trusting Sophia to help keep the house tidy and not to pry. She started to join in the domestic routine, washing up and occasionally doing some of the cooking, with supplies from the big freezer and the well-stocked kitchen cabinets. Once she did yield to temptation while he was out, and tried to turn on his laptop, but the big beast was password-protected, and she got no further than the login screen. Without the internet, her main mental stimulants were Carvill's books, which were scattered all round the cabin, in bookcases, shelves, desk and table spaces, and even unfiled stacks, neatly pushed out of the way against the walls. Carvill's library seemed to alternate oddly between alphabetical and subject order. Her gaze wandered over the Bs: Ballard, Bataille, Bierce, Burroughs. Then on to one of the most substantial sections, on beliefs and history of religion. Most impressive was a complete twelve-volume set of Frazer's original *The Golden Bough* in gold-lettered green bindings, but there was also a three-volume facsimile of the Florentine Codex, and many other works of mythology and ethnography, some of them less famous and even less welcome: one on the Jonestown Massacre, another on *Nameless Cults;* occult works by Crowley and Yeats. None of that seemed to chime with the intensely physical, imagistic verse of his earlier sonnets. Carvill apparently had been delving into fringe beliefs and curious sects. At least he hadn't become some cult leader with a stable of nubile disciples out here in the backwoods, though she knew there were enough Carvill groupies out there to fuel any commune.

Carvill showed no apparent interest in her choice of reading or how she spent her time when he was out of the house, so long as she stuck to his restrictions on trying to call out or access the internet; sometimes he would leave the study door locked, sometimes standing open. She came across nothing in the room worth investigating anyway, without the login for his laptop, and there was not even a Wifi network in the place, just a fixed link that led to a landline router somewhere up out of sight in the cabin roof. Of course there was no reason for Carvill to be interested in her thought processes, but his calm indifference nettled her.

"Is this really a safe place to keep your books and papers?" she needled him. "I mean, you're out here in the middle of nowhere, in a highly inflammable pine building, miles from the nearest fire station. Anything could happen. Think of T.E. Lawrence's manuscript, or Byron's memoirs."

"Oh, you think I've got them here, do you?" he chuckled, raising an eyebrow. They were sitting together on folding garden chairs outside the house, in a specially deep patch of shade, basking drowsily in the warmth of midday, a bottle of Bushmills and two tumblers on the table in between them.

She nodded, her head wobbling slightly on her neck, woozy and a little buzzed by the heat and the whiskey. She wore a cotton summer dress, one of the few she had brought with her, light and easy wear for the June heat, and right now it was clinging to her armpits and the backs of her knees, making her itch. "In a place like this, so full of treasures, I'm willing to bet on it, Desmond Carvill. No fear of the media tracking you down and ransacking your private stash; yeah, I think you keep your memories here."

"You're sure of yourself, girl. And I like your deductive logic. Well, what if I did? Is that what you came here for?"

"Of course," she countered, glossing over the confusion that his question suddenly awoke in her. "Do you think I'd have accepted this white elephant deal of yours otherwise?"

"Well, if that's how it is, that's how it is." He paused for a moment and looked up into the leaf cover. "I guess I'd better let you see them then."

Suddenly stone cold sober, she looked at him. "I was joking, you know," she faltered. "Do you really have them here?"

Carvill nodded. "Sure, I know you were. But yes I do have them here. And perhaps it is time I let you have a look at them." He fished into the back pocket of his jeans, where she knew he kept a keyring on a coiled flex clipped to a belt loop, and unclipped the ring. "There you go," he announced, holding it out to her. "It's the big Chubb key with the red enamel on the bow. Take it."

She stood up awkwardly. To take the key, she had to reach across the table. The thick honeyed air of the summer day, with the dust motes turning in sunbeams between the branches and the faint murmur of birds and bees, seemed to resist and impede her, as if she was trapped in amber already. "Go on, take it," he urged, pushing it towards her. She took the keyring and slipped the keys between her fingers until she was pinching the red-painted one.

"Where…?" she asked.

"The locked door next to the larder," he supplied. "There's a short passage and another door at the end, but the padlock's not shut right now. Just be sure to close both doors while you're in there, and when you leave: they need constant temperature and humidity." She nodded, and left him sipping his whiskey, still gazing up at the sun-dappled leaves overhead.

Sophia still had no clear picture of the overall layout of Carvill's rambling estate. The encircling trees hid the fences and borders of the property, and the outbuildings receded among them and disappeared between their trunks. Weatherboarded corridors and covered walkways between the shacks and lean-to sheds only confused her mental map even further; for all she knew, there could have been any number of secret chambers, or even halls, opening off the front rooms.

The door off the entrance to the pantry opened into a short, enclosed corridor lit by one small perspex skylight, sloping rather steeply downhill with a similar door at the far end, rather like a pinewood airlock. She closed the door behind her as bidden, and opened the other one, noticing a padlock hanging open from the drawn bolt. The room beyond was even dimmer, and she had to blink and adjust her eyes to the gloom at first before she could make out the interior.

The chamber was octagonal, higher than it was wide, like a lantern or a chapter house in some medieval cathedral. Narrow niche windows illuminated it, but these weren't glazed: rather, they seemed to let the daylight in through very thin parchments or hides. The dim amber glow was hardly enough to see by, so she flicked on the lights. Twin spots played down on two wooden pillars in the center of the room, each supporting a single open book under its own bell jar like a specimen of Victorian taxidermy. She stepped closer, gingerly, craning over the paler of the two books. There, sure enough, was Carvill's Sonnet #7 from *Daphnia*, inscribed in beautiful reddish script on the bone-colored page, the same shade as the rubrics in a medieval illuminated manuscript. And on the other pillar reposed *Nyx*, darker toned, as she had been told. These were the original two books.

Could she touch them, examine them? she wondered. Carvill had said nothing about keeping her hands off, and the glass jars seemed easy enough to lift, with no screws or wires to secure them. There were no other lights beside the spotlights and a ring of uplighters near the pyramidal ceiling, and especially no blinking lights for an alarm system, no security cameras that she could see, even though the books themselves must have been worth tens of thousands of dollars at the very least. No temperature dial or hiss of air conditioning either; Carvill obviously believed that books, like wine, should be kept under natural conditions and at natural temperatures. She decided to chance it, and lifted the bell jar carefully off *Daphnia*, placing it on the carpeted floor because there was no other surface or worktop or chair in the room. With the slightly dusty glass canopy off, the book's pages looked even brighter and newer, and Sophia lifted the corner of the right-hand leaf with the tip of her fingernail, leaning over to drink in the words. As she had expected, there was not a single sign of underdrawing or advance preparation on the vellum: every penstroke seemed to have been made with the same unhesitating grace as Carvill had shown when inscribing her name. She read the familiar words eagerly; her hopes of following Carvill's tempo of composition and creation rather dashed by the limpid perfection of his penmanship, but also put into their true perspective by the beautiful object at her fingertips. With no other fittings in the room, no desk or table to rest the book on, she pored over *Daphnia* as though she was meditating on it in a cloister, captivated by its pages. Then, for she had no idea whether Carvill would ever give her another opportunity, she did the same to *Nyx*.

With the light starting to fade outside the windows, she replaced the two glass domes and left the two relics behind her, closing the inner door and locking the outer one. She found Carvill in almost exactly the same position she had left him, still holding his tumbler.

"Well, what did you think?" he asked, glancing up at her quizzically.

She poured another swig of whiskey and downed it, then sat down before answering, uncertain what to say and still a little unsteady on her feet, amid the mesmeric hum of the bees in the warm afternoon. Her shoulders felt stiff from so long bent over the pages.

"They're incredible," she breathed at last. "Not what I expected at all. It's hard to know what to say."

He nodded. "You have to experience them hands on. Anything else is just an echo. All those writers, critics, and publishers prating that all words are the same, wherever they're written or printed: it's not so."

"Then you're denying them to the world," she objected quietly, not wanting to challenge him on that point, but feeling compelled to state it, or maybe it was the liquor talking. "Like an improvisation or a dance piece, they're a one-time-only thing. Without a recording, there's nothing but a hint or a memory."

Carvill took a short sip of Bushmills. "The world has as much of an echo as it can ever get," he asserted. "The moment you left the exhibition hall, it would be the same. Facsimile, scan, it's never the same. Like Blake's illuminated books: unless you hold the originals in your hands, you'll never experience the actual physical reality. Oh, when I'm gone, I'll gift them to the NYPL or somewhere, but," he paused reflectively for a moment, "while I'm here, I want the girls here with me."

She looked at him: did he mean the girls who inspired the two collections, or the books themselves? Moved by a moment's tenderness, she leaned across the table and rested her hand on the back of his, where it clutched the tumbler of Bushmills. He looked sidelong at her, put down the glass, and squeezed her hand in return.

Carvill was closer to her now, so much so that when John drove in with a fresh batch of supplies, it felt almost like an intrusion. Was it the seventh morning? The eighth? Anyway, the next day Carvill woke her early with a knock on the door of her room and invited her to join him on his morning hike. Sophia dressed in the same light jacket she had worn for the ride up, wondering if her sneakers would be enough for the forest trails. Carvill wore his khaki ranger vest over his habitual dark t-shirt, jeans and walking boots, with an unmounted sniperscope in its case jammed into the vest's lower pocket. The weather was the same changeless, balmy summer daze, almost windless under the trees.

Carvill led her down his habitual track towards the forest behind the house, past the maze of outbuildings, stilll just as confusing from this angle, and into the trees. There was no fence, post, sign, or other mark of human habitation in the wood beyond the bare earth trail, which might as easily have been worn by animal as by human feet. Soon they had left any sight of the house behind, and Sophia noticed that the forest was beginning to open up, letting in more light between the trunks. Clearings started to appear, both beside the path and further off in the woods.

They passed a little enclosure off the path, with a shingled roof on posts covering a wooden platform which supported four large logs stood on end, with clefts in their sides. A gentle droning rose from the logs, and occasional bees flew in and out.

"Those are bee gums," Carvill explained. "I keep my own bees. The logs are hollow and the bees live inside them, old style. Maybe one day I'll harvest my own honey, but I don't want to drive them out of their hives."

"And what's that?" she asked a few minutes later, pointing towards a crude wooden ladder scaffold leaning against a tree.

"Deer blind," he explained. "It gives me a clear view over… this."

As he finished, the trees gave out, and they found themselves at the crest of a miniature ridge, just a few splinters of Adirondack rock, opening up a prospect beyond the enclosing woods to the true mountains. There was a short grassy slope below their vantage point, dotted with bushes and ground cover, then another treeline just a short distance away. Beyond the clearing, in every direction, more forested hills stretched away, then further ranges of wooded peaks beyond them, immense, uniform, endless.

"Wow," she breathed, "we really are in the wilds. Is this all yours?"

"We passed into public land a few minutes back," he chuckled, though apparently a little subdued. "The Forest Preserve is still open for hunting, though. And nobody bothers to check very carefully up here. I haven't seen a Forest Ranger in weeks."

"Oh," she murmured, moving a little closer to him involuntarily. Thank God for the slight wind and the occasional bird calls; otherwise she would have found the stillness and solitude overpowering.

"You should see it in autumn," he breathed. "The colors are incredible."

Was that an invitation, she wondered. "I doubt I'll be here that long," she demurred. He looked at her cryptically, then nodded as though something in her expression had confirmed his thoughts.

"Come on, let's get some breakfast," he said, and led her gently away. They held hands all the way back.

Sophia knew what was coming all the rest of the afternoon. The atmosphere between them was electric with that static charge from rubbing together, stronger than summer thunder. Dinner that evening was a feast of expectation, only a light meal so as not to slow or weigh them down too much, but every moment savored. At the end, they stacked the dirty dishes in the sink together, side by side, then turned towards each other and started kissing.

Carvill smelt of male sweat from the heat of the day, meat, and pinewood. His craftsman's fingers put great, precise force into their tips as they probed and teased her shoulders, her collarbones, her breasts, jointing her, finding each point of juncture in her body and probing at it until she felt as unstrung as a puppet or a doll. He drew her into his bedroom by both arms, that very masculine room she had only glimpsed into till now, then pushed her brusquely back on the bed. She half lay there, watching him unbelt his jeans and pull his tee up and off his body.

Years of outdoor life and all those handicrafts had left Carvill tanned and hard, tauter and better muscled than any younger man she had been with. Despite Gaye's urging, Sophia had done little to keep in shape, and beside Carvill, she felt very soft, very unfinished, very adolescent, as she let him take off her tank top and jeans, unfasten her bra, then quickly roll to the bedside to slip on a condom. But it had been so long. And he was so hard.

Once inside, he thrust aggressively, harshly, maybe because he had been up here so long by himself in the woods. She clung to him as the bed creaked beneath them, gasping, still stroking and feeling that matte white Irish skin with the freckle spots, finding enough strength of her own to wrap her legs around his driving hips and pull him deeper into her. When he withdrew, he left her bruised and sore, wet, aching, unsatisfied, still yearning. She sat up in bed, put her arms round his shoulders and leaned her cheek against his corded back.

"Thank you," she breathed, kissing his freckled shoulder blades.

"It's me who should be thanking you," his voice rumbled in his chest, but he kept his head turned away. "Sorry if I was a wee bit rough that time."

"It's alright," she sighed, nuzzling against him. "I don't mind."

"You'll be needing another, then," he laughed under his breath. "Just give me a few here. Need to rest and recoup just a bit"

She slipped around his body, and carefully slid the condom off him with both hands, pinching it shut. "As soon as you want me," she smiled, rubbing herself catlike against his thighs.

———

After that, they were like any new couple, teasing, playing, experimenting, laughing. Carvill's age didn't seem to matter: it took away juvenile male anxiety and insecurity without slowing him down. When they weren't making love, they would talk casually about ordinary matters or nothing at all, only rarely about literature. Sophia wondered if she should worry about that. Should she be probing him, interrogating him? Was she a scholar still, or a groupie now? Or what? Did she even care?

One thing she did notice was that Carvill practised his calligraphy and craftwork almost daily, like a virtuoso exercising his scales; sometimes lines of other writers' poetry or prose, at other times just single words. At times, he would work on paper with a fountain pen, but mostly he seemed to focus on his leatherwork with his blunt-ended knife. Sophia welcomed that: it kept his hands nimble and his strength up, sustained the well-toned poise that turned his physical assertiveness into a dance, so that even when he was pushing her head down onto him, it felt as though he was moulding her.

"Don't you write anymore?" she asked one evening, kissing along the edge of his ribcage.

"Oh, you're wanting me to put you in a poem, are you?" he chuckled throatily, looking down at her.

"What you do is your own business, Mister Carvill," she answered nonchalantly, with another kiss, then another. "I was just asking, that's all."

"I only write at the end of relationships," he continued, with a sudden tightness in his voice, looking away. She glanced up at him.

"Does that apply to me?" She was unable to keep the catch out of her throat.

"It's not what you think," he replied, looking down at her and squeezing the nape of her slender neck. "I don't mean it that way."

"Then what way do you mean it?" she pressed, lifting her lips from him and propping herself up on her elbows. "Are you going to just pack me off back to NYU and call it a day: wham, bam, thank you Ma'am, and no kiss and tell? Is that how it works?"

"Well, that was the arrangement," he said, turning his head aside again.

Tears starting unbidden from her eyes, she started beating at his chest with her small fists. "You bastard," she sobbed. "You ghoul. How dare you use me like that?"

Carvill seized her wrists, seemingly more to calm her than because of any pain. "I told you, it's not like that," he said intently, pushing his face into hers. "Will you listen to me?"

Surprised by the intensity of his gaze, she quietened and looked up at him.

"Now I ask you to remember the agreement you made and how ye got here," he urged, his brogue thickening with the intensity of his voice. "I'm trusting you, and you're bound to secrecy. Do ye understand?"

Silently, she nodded.

"Come with me, then." He pulled her up out of the bed and led her, stark naked, out of the bedroom and to the back of the cabin. Indoors, in the warm evening, there was no discomfort or chill in being naked, but she still felt vulnerable, the more so because Carvill seemed completely, almost unnaturally, at ease in his nakedness. He unlocked the back door to the little reliquary annex, and pulled her down the short corridor to the far end, still unbolted. Once inside, he let go of her arm, switched on the lights, and turned to face her.

"Now," he said, gesturing towards the glowing books that stood out even more strongly against the last fading illumination from the windows. "I told you that my girls, who were here before you, are still here, didn't I? Well, there they are. I've never left them, and I've never forgotten or forsaken them."

"What are you trying to tell me?" she asked, shivering slightly despite the room's steady ambient temperature. Carvill gave one very slightly sardonic sniff at her choice of words.

"I got closer to them than any other man could," he explained patiently, encompassing both books with a single sweep of his naked, well-muscled arm.

"How?" she asked, though already she had such a clear idea of what he was going to tell her that the question was almost a formality.

Carvill paused for just one moment, like a diver taking his breath before plunging into the water.

"I skinned them both alive. They knew what was coming, and they both accepted it. Because they understood. They gave themselves fully, into my hands, to be made immortal, my precious material, my medium, for eternity."

Sophia nodded. So that's it, she thought numbly, bizarrely, reflecting with equal objectivity that she must be in shock.

"Why?" she asked, with barely enough breath to complete the question.

Carvill spread his big, capable hands helplessly, but more in an admission of incompetence than of guilt. "It's the only thing that will get me there. I can't reach the peak of my talent without it. I hardly know what I'm doing while I do it, but once it's done, the words are there."

"And nothing else works?" she probed, perfectly ready to interrogate him now, with her feelings temporarily knocked out of commission.

"You think I didn't try? I tried every way I could: tattoo sessions, drugs, grafts. It just didn't work. I couldn't fool my own mind, no matter how I tried."

She nodded, comprehension dawning. "The third book," she breathed.

"Exactly. I know how crap it is. I tried. That was the result. Hardly seems worth the bother, does it? So here I am, back at square one."

"I can't tell anyone else now, can I?" she asked.

He shook his head.

"I'm sorry, but we won't let you tell. Of course, you could go to the police, but then who would believe you? You don't know where you are, and even if you do find out, remember William Burroughs. He never stood trial. Besides, you know this was offered to you, in a gesture of trust. I'm in your hands."

His hazel green eyes fixed again on hers, and she trembled and lowered her gaze. His own hands looked perfectly able to wring the life out of her if he chose, but she felt fairly sure that that at least wasn't going to happen.

"And Grace Weather?"

"She knows my terms, but not why. At most, she may suspect that something happened to the girls, but not what it was. It's all on me."

"This is what happened to that girl in Texas, isn't it?" she remarked flatly.

"She was the only other one who ever got this far," he confirmed. "I know where she is now. She went back after her time here, on the same terms, but she couldn't handle what she'd learned. The critics think it was the work that did it, but no, I know it wasn't. It was the guilt. I'm truly sorry for that, but I can't help what happened to her after she left me."

Carvill massaged his face wearily. *Now what do I do? Sophia wondered. Do I go mad like her? What happens to my career?*

"I need a moment." She blinked, and stole one last glance at the two books behind him, resplendent and serene on their plinths, then staggered out of the chamber and back up to her room, where she pulled the robe around her shoulders and sat curled up on a small wooden chair, staring at the wall. She had never again expected to feel as alone as she had in her childhood, but Carvill had confounded her.

She heard him approach after an indefinite amount of time, unhurried and deliberate. One chill flicker of fear told her for a moment that she should dress and run, but to where? She felt no danger from him, and that fearful instant was more the cold voice of reason speaking than anything her heart told her. He knocked gently at the bedroom door, though it was already ajar. She raised her head to see him standing in the doorway, already back in his t-shirt and jeans.

"I would like you to see something else, if you can handle it now," he said in a low voice. "It might help you understand."

She looked at him, receptive to whatever he had to propose, though still dazed.

"Before it happened, the girls made their last testaments, as well as some kind of explanation. Oh, and as parting gifts for me, just in case, for some possible reduction of sentence." He chuckled, still the old Desmond Carvill. "I wouldn't force anything on anyone. I want you to know that. They wanted the world to know that too. Will you come and see?"

Sophia nodded, still uncertain what if anything she could say to him. Carvill stood aside and let her walk to his study without touching her, lifted the lid of the big laptop, and tapped in his password one-handed. Soon he had a media player screen open for her.

"I'll leave you with her," he said, withdrawing.

Sophia pressed play. A lovely black girl appeared onscreen, dressed in a singlet, thick bubbly curls and voluptuous curves contrasting with her composed, intent expression. The video had been filmed in semi-darkness, with most of the illumination on the girl, but Sophia guessed from what she could see of the background that it had been recorded almost exactly where she was sitting now.

After giving her name and her social security number, the girl declared, slowly and clearly, that she was not under the influence of drugs or alcohol and was making the statement of her own free will. She said that Carvill had explained to her in full what would happen, and that she would not survive, but she was prepared, and ready for "as much immortality as anyone can get for sure these days." She said nothing about family at the end, but sent her best wishes to anyone who remembered her, and assured them, "I'll always be with you."

Sophia blinked through tears at the empty square where the girl had been, that black girl who had been the inspiration for *Nyx*, whose skin was now bound in the volume in Carvill's octagonal chamber, bearing his deathless verses to her. That book with its dark vellum leaves, cut out of her flesh.

"That was it," said Carvill, once again at the doorway, back far enough not to block her exit or loom over her. "Are you okay?"

"I wish I smoked, because I feel like I need a cigarette," she sniffed, with a little wan smile. He regarded her calmly, all the nervous tension gone now that he was dressed again and in command of himself. His composure was oddly reassuring, the calm center of a dark storm. She couldn't help but be drawn to it.

"Come on, I think you've had enough for one night," he said, and held out his hand. She took it without thinking, and once she was on his feet, he hugged her. She leaned against him, needing the closeness, the physical contact, the emotional support she had never felt as a child. Carvill was the only one there to reach out to. He rocked her in his arms.

"Here, let me put you to bed." He led her back to her own room, laid her down in her bed, and kissed her forehead. The emotional strain had exhausted her, and immediately she fell asleep, closing her eyes against all the questions and fears.

⁓

Next morning was another changeless summer day, heralded by the smell of bacon and coffee as Carvill cooked for her. He brought breakfast to her on a tray, knowing her tastes well enough by now to make what she liked best, and she found she had a good appetite. He sat beside her on the edge of the bed and watched her while she ate.

"I thought you'd need that," he observed coolly.

"Oh, you've done this before?" she quipped, as she chewed.

"Now now, I'm no Bluebeard," he chuckled, deep in his chest. "I told you the truth."

"I know you did," she nodded. "Don't think that makes it any better." Somehow she had gained composure, poise to match his own from last night, perhaps because she knew that what he said was true, including the fact that she did now have power over him, whatever the danger. Obviously Carvill knew that too, and he accepted it calmly as the cost of revelation. There was a certain honor in that, she reflected.

"You took a hell of a risk bringing me here like this," she remarked.

Carvill shrugged. "Better than being alone here for the rest of my life. Besides, I wouldn't have brought you here unless I thought I could trust you. And maybe it's the confessional itch; I can't have this on me without sharing someday."

"Oh, glad to be of service," she quipped, feeling like she was still fencing with him in that loving cut and thrust of parry and riposte. "You're a giver, I see."

"Always," he smiled at her, with exactly the same warm tenderness he had always shown. She couldn't help smiling back at him. This was unreal, how calm and intimate they were, but then again, wasn't the whole situation unreal? Was she really here, or would she wake up one morning to find she had never left her room and had dreamt the whole thing? "So, what happens now?" she asked, offhand.

"You stay here," he responded. "There's no time limit now. I can give you email access, to make any arrangements you still need to make. Did you tell anyone when you'd be back?"

She shook her head, all frank openness. "Study leave, I said. Didn't give a return date. They'll be expecting me back at the beginning of the next semester, but I didn't say one way or the other."

He reached across and squeezed her hand; she squeezed back.

After that, they settled back into the old groove: cooking, walking, making love, watching the deer in the woods. Sophia's occasional urge to bolt added a thrill, an urgency, to even the innocuous forest walks. Carvill's manner towards her hadn't changed, he was still the same old forceful, demanding lover, and she found she could push back against him with aggression born of fear, sometimes biting his shoulder or clawing his back and even drawing blood. Payback, she mused, reminding herself that she was lying next to a murderer. No, that wasn't what he was. So what was he? A suicider? An assisted killer? She had no idea. Meanwhile, Carvill kept up his craftwork with the same dedication, though now she could read more into his knifestrokes on the hide.

"Would you do that with me?" she asked casually one morning, watching him tool another square of leather.

"You asking?" He stopped and looked up at her.

"Yes," she nodded, challenging.

Carvill put down stretcher and tool on the workbench, turned, and took her in his arms in one smooth motion.

"I wouldn't do anything so crude," he declared, holding her. "I'd draw off some blood to help tint the ink. Then I'd tattoo the lines on your skin: shoulder blades, upper arms, back, breasts, stomach, hips, thighs." He brushed each place on her body as he spoke. "Then I'd lift the skin off, in panels."

She met his green gaze. "Is that what you did with the others?"

He nodded. "I could inscribe the lines on your dead hide, but where would be the intimacy, the passion, the communion, in that? Only this can get me there. You do understand, don't you?" He looked down at her, ran his callused thumbs up and down her bare arms, and actually started quoting Scripture at her. "For this corruptible must put on incorruption, and this mortal must put on immortality. So when this corruptible shall have put on incorruption, and this mortal shall have put on immortality, then shall be brought to pass the saying that is written, Death is swallowed up in victory. O death, where is thy sting? O grave, where is thy victory?"

"Oh, no sting?" she half chuckled. "Are you saying it won't hurt?"

"Oh, no. It's agonizing. Until the shock kicks in. Then you won't feel a thing."

"You're joking, right?" Despite herself, she managed an ironic smile. Suddenly she found herself discussing such atrocious things so easily, so naturally.

"Well, okay, if you're pushing me." He smiled sheepishly and looked down for a moment. "Yes you'll feel something. But not like the pain itself. A different sensation."

"I think I'd be disappointed otherwise." Had that really come out of her mouth? Once she got into the groove of a certain banter with him, it was so hard to snap herself out of it again. "I certainly wouldn't trust you if you told me I'd feel nothing at all."

"So it's about trust now, is it?" he chided.

"No, I trust you." She kissed him. With the close air and warm sunbeams in that pine building, with its scent of earth and wood oils, and his body against hers, it was so hard to think clearly, and the only way she could see to go was to push forward. "I don't know."

"Yes you do."

Carvill led her back to the house and they made love again, and again, in the fresh air blowing in through the open windows, swathed in sweat from the heat that they didn't bother to wash off. Then, after so much hard, aggressive sex, as the light was beginning to fade from the sky, he got up, and pulled her out of bed and across the front room to his study.

"Here you go," he said, sitting her down on the desk chair and turning the laptop on. "Say your piece."

"Could I have a t-shirt, please?" she asked. He smiled indulgently, and fetched her one from his room, then logged in on the machine for her.

Left alone, Sophia looked at her image in the laptop's webcam before she began. Now, dressed in the oversized tee, she looked more together, more composed, more centered, than she'd ever been. Besides, where else could she go now, knowing what she knew? So she sat down and looked straight into the camera lens, and said her piece.

Their last night of lovemaking was as angry and aggressive as before, but Sophia felt constantly on the verge of tears, with a breathless, delirious sadness that only heightened the excitement. She clung to Carvill, gnawed at him, left tears and sweat and bruises on his shoulders, filled by him now repeatedly, laughing at the ludicrous idea of protection. Besides, he had caught her just at the right point in her cycle, ironically, just as she was about to bleed. She did sleep a little, exhausted, and wandered through dark, formless dreams that vanished without leaving a memory when he shook her gently awake with dawn light stealing in through the windows.

"Go take a shower," he instructed her, quietly but firmly. Obediently, she went to the bathroom and showered, soaping herself clean and fragrant, and quickly rinsing her hair. When she returned to the bedroom, Carvill was already dressed in his usual t-shirt and jeans. He untied her robe, slipped it off her, unwound the towel round her hair, and led her naked and barefoot out to the workshop, across the yard, the earth yielding under her feet and the morning air cool on her skin, without bothering to close the front door of the house. She was terrified, but she couldn't deny a certain bizarre excitement, anticipation even.

Once in the workshop, he did close the door, then pulled a huge stretcher frame away from the wall, and stood it in the middle of the floor, securing it with cabling to eyebolts in the roofbeams. He took her by the hands and positioned her in the middle of it, then fastened her wrists to the upper corners and her ankles to the lower with thongs, stretching her like a St. Andrew's cross, but steady on the ground, with enough flexion to move a little and hang slightly from the straps. Her eyes widened as he brought out two glass jars, each with a clear plastic tube emerging from the top, tipped by a long, large-bore needle.

"Shh, this part really isn't so bad," he reassured her, noticing the fear in her eyes, and kissed her gently on the cheek. Then he stuck first one needle, then the other, into her upper thighs, and bright arterial blood started to flow down the tubes into the jars. He was right about the pain: it was no worse than she remembered from blood drives. Carvill looked down at the jars and watched, occasionally squeezing her wrist, until both were half full, then pulled out the needles and applied an amber waxen ointment to staunch the bleeding from each thigh.

"Honey cream," he explained. "A mixture of beeswax, honey, and flour. Sweets to the sweet." Then he kissed her again. She nodded groggily, already a little light-headed from the loss of blood, and kissed him back. He scuffed over a few drops of spilt blood on the floor with a foot, and Sophia reflected that he'd dig the floor over once he was done, to hide the blood. She noticed that he was already more detached, aloof, a mantle of almost trancelike calm settling over him, and she guessed he must be entering the fugue state he needed to compose his poems.

Carvill took the lids off the two jars and poured in some other crimson liquid from a plastic bottle, mixing the solution with a stick until a brighter red, thinner fluid filled each jar. Then he drew off some of the ink into a small rack of little cups, and dipped into it with a needle-tipped device like a drawing pen with a double-barreled hilt, at the end of a long thin electric flex. He pulled its trigger, and a wasplike buzzing filled the workshop. Staring at her with fixed, almost manic concentration, Carvill started on her breasts.

Sophia flinched at first at the incessant stinging that just went on and on, until she began to drift off into her own fugue, swaying from the straps, feeling a glow settle over her whole body. Carvill wove around her like a matador, balanced on the balls of his feet, pricking her first in one place and then another, until the warm glow was everywhere, enfolding her. Head loose on her shoulders, she looked down at Carvill, noticing with the shrinking part of her brain that could still sustain something like detached clarity that his eyes were locked on her body, seeming to drill into the flesh deeper than the tattoo needle, mapping every contour and feature, and he seemed to be mumbling to himself, perhaps subvocalizing the poems he was inscribing on her skin. The tingling all over her body seemed one with the buzzing of the tattoo gun. Sweat started to pour down her body as she hung from the frame. Carvill paused now and again to wipe away the sweat and the blood and the pinkish lymph weeping from her skin, and occasionally give her a sip of sports drink from a bicycle bottle. By the time he reached her thighs, she was floating in a haze of detached bliss, no longer herself, only the faintest curiosity left about what he had written on her.

Finally, he straightened up and put down his tattoo gun, then moved it and the jars aside, and lifted over a low side table of flat trays, with more gauze sheets and bottles, to stand beside her.

"This part will be quick, I promise," he told her, finally looking her in the eye with his fixed, green gaze. "Do you forgive me?"

"I forgive you," she mumbled, and kissed him back when he kissed her. Then Carvill took up a short knife with a walnut handle and broad curved blade, and went round behind her back.

The first cut was not how she expected: no sharp pain but a broad intensification of the same tingling, buzzing feeling over her shoulders, pushing at her back, and with it an intensification of the rapt, detached feeling that lifted her out of herself almost as though he had given her angel's wings. Then the pain came full force as she felt him slice under the top layer of skin and peel the first panels off, laying them down in the waiting trays, where she could dimly discern raised lines of red script under the draining blood. Carvill seemed to move to a drumbeat, until she realized the drumbeat was her own pulse thundering in her temples – and was that sighing and howling of wind her own screams and gasps? When he had finished with her back and arms, he cut more broadly and pulled harder: he's taking the rest off, the neat, precise, detached observer in the echoing dome of her skull told her. Once he started on her breasts, her head flopped down, and she watched with a glazed fascination as he peeled them like a pair of ripe fruit to reveal the juicy pulp under the rind. Occasionally, he darted a compassionate glance up at her as she hung there, and when his head was down level with her groin, he kissed her mound before he took her skin away.

At last the fourteen panels lay in their waiting trays, ready for cleaning, treating, and binding. Sophia realized that she now wore her face like a mask or hood over a peeled red form, all its parts laid bare, needing only a few more cuts and pulls to be completely naked. He kissed her one last time. Then his body pressed against her excoriated flesh, and she could bear his touch no more.

Epilogue

Desmond Carvill's third book, *Hypatia*, appeared to universal acclaim, tinged with some relief among the loyalists who could at last hail a return to his full peerless form. A third sonnet cycle like the two preceding classics, *Hypatia* didn't even need its epigraph from the author, "This is my third book," to reassure readers that Carvill was back at the height of his powers. Grace Weather, cryptic as ever, gave away no details about its composition, and refused all questions, but evidently there had been a new muse behind it, whose sweet yet sophisticated character suffused its imagery. Critics spotted the obvious allusion to Hypatia of Alexandria, and speculated that Carvill was commemorating that martyred secular saint of wisdom, scholarship, and female equality. But the same old sensual rapture was still there, undiminished and anything but intellectual. Whoever she had been, reviewers agreed, the living, breathing woman behind *Hypatia* had drawn new capabilities out of Carvill, layered new strata of significance and force into his pellucid verse. The same old rumors and conspiracy theories proliferated. Few readers could agree anything about the actual woman behind *Hypatia*, except that she must have been some kind of goddess to inspire such miraculous lines. Some wondered if they could expect a fourth book.

Amid all the furor of the new publication, the disappearance of one graduate student attracted little notice. Sophia's teachers guessed she had just dropped out, or burned out, another casualty of the Carvill myth. If only she had held on long enough for the third sonnet cycle, things might have turned out differently, but with the fresh impetus just given to Carvill studies, there were plenty more up-and-coming students to fill her shoes.

Gaye guessed that her bestie must have found the same bliss that she was now enjoying, hidden away somewhere with Carvill in his ivory tower. Maybe someday she would hear from her again. Meantime, she had her first-edition copy of *Hypatia* to hold in her hand, read, marvel at, and wonder if Sophia had at last found her dream and become a divine Muse, an apotheosis in words, as she squeezed her ribcage between her arms in a little private hug.

Afterword

This extended love letter to New York is a wistful look back at that cultural Mecca from the far side of the abyss. Sophia Amory embodies that city's, and America's, literary heritage. I cringe at the recrudescence of other, far less attractive, strains in (and stains on) America's heritage since I started kicking round the initial conception back in December 2016, and I don't think I'll be back in New York until they're laid to rest. But the book isn't about them. At the time of writing, this is a compilation of dreams and memory.

Dark and horrible things happen to Sophia in the course of the story, but those were not intended as any kind of socio-political critique of the assault on America's highest values and traditions. Instead, this is more a story of individual depression and deception (by self and other). Needless to say (I hope), this book does not endorse violence against women. Rather, it can be read as an elaborate warning against predators, especially those who are idolized, empowered, and rendered unaccountable by adoring cliques and subcultures. And I've seen enough of such behaviour, especially in the BDSM community, for all its self-policing pretensions, to feel I know it by heart.

Desmond Carvill was set up as the whipping boy (no pun intended) for this phenomenon, and to encapsulate my assault on the whole misbegotten hagiography of the Artist as Hero/Prophet/Savant/Saint/Superman/Whatever.

There's not a little satire in here. Carvill's art is his alibi. Instead of being an artist who has developed psychopathic tendencies, he is a charismatic psychopath who has developed an artistic cover. And he has worked so hard on his cover story that he has actually lifted it into the realm of great art: after all, it's part of his battery of techniques for luring his prey. It's also his cunning play on the vacuous adoration of the Artist by Manhattanites, and by shallow culturati everywhere. Carvill is a textbook strong narcissistic personality. And he is the most insidious and calculating of ambush predators. Some first readers felt I should exhibit less loathing and contempt for him: after all, he's a creation of my own mind, and presumably reflects a part of me. But I don't see any reason to detest him any less.

Finally, after a very, very few initial hesitations, I wrote *The Three Books* deliberately excluding any supernatural element. I wanted to write a purely psychological horror story that still had enough of a flavour of the unknown, the inexplicable, the mysterious and bizarre, without wandering into occult territory. Hopefully I've succeeded; I certainly tried. *The Three Books* nods towards Pascal Laugier's *Martyrs* far more than it does towards Roman Polanski's *The Ninth Gate*, but even then, there's no final suggestion of transcendence. I do have a specific ideological beef about occultism, due to its long inglorious association with fascism of all stripes and similar anti-rationalist creeds, and I've written a lot more about that elsewhere. Hopefully again, that hasn't overburdened the story. I did write it partly to try to recover for psychological horror and mystery some of the flavour, suggestiveness and ontological gravity found more often in supernatural and weird fiction.

Thanks to Sarah Carter, Director at the Bridwell Art Library in Kentucky, for some leads regarding art books. Thanks to old friend and tattoo artist Ee Koon Goh for her advice on tattooing. Thanks to John Langan, for his early praise for this story and his general marvellousness. Thanks also to Steve Shaw, my publisher, for taking a chance on publishing the story.

I dedicate this book to Krystyne, my unfailingly insightful (and unpaid) editor, who was really responsible for getting me to tone down my habitual vices and bring this story to its full potential. And to my Cenobite Muse, who inspired the tale, and turned me on to Netflix in time to gorge on *Jessica Jones* and *Daredevil*; and who got me over to the States in the long hot summer of 2016, to read in Baltimore and at Bluestockings in the Lower East Side, and to attend the H.P. Lovecraft Film Festival & CthulhuCon in Providence, RI. And to a very wonderful princess, who knows exactly what she means to me. And to my parents and my daughters, always.

Paul StJohn Mackintosh
20 January 2018

Paul StJohn Mackintosh is a Scottish poet, writer of weird fiction, translator and journalist. Born in 1961, he was educated at Trinity College, Cambridge, has lived and worked in Asia and Central Europe, and currently divides his time between Hungary and other locations.

Paul's first collection of dark/weird/transgressive fiction, *Black Propaganda*, appeared from H. Harksen Productions in May 2016. His second story collection, *The Echo of The Sea & Other Strange War Stories*, was published by Egaeus Press in October 2017. His short story 'The People of the Island,' in *Eldritch Horrors: Dark Tales*, from H. Harksen Productions, received an Honorable Mention from Ellen Datlow in her 'Best Horror of the Year Volume Two' list for 2009. His acclaimed first poetry collection, *The Golden Age*, was published by Bellew Publishing in 1997, and reissued on Kindle in 2013, and his second poetry collection, *The Musical Box of Wonders*, was published by H. Harksen Productions in 2011. His Lovecraftian and dark fiction has appeared in several formats and journals worldwide, and his co-translations from the Japanese, done with Maki Sugiyama, include *The Poems of Nakahara Chuya* (1993) and *Nip the Buds, Shoot the Kids* (1995) by the 1994 Nobel Prize-winner

Kenzaburo Oe, which won a Japan Festival Award. He translated the poems for the Japanese photo-travelogue and exhibition catalogue *Utamakura* (Asuka Historical Museum, 1998). He also co-translated *Superstrings* (2007) by Dinu Flamand from Romanian with Olga Dunca.

Paul is an Associate Editor for the US books, publishing and literary website Teleread.org, writing regularly on cultural and publishing matters, and has been rated #1 of "The 12 Publishing Shakers You Should Be Following" by *The Independent Publishing Magazine*. He writes and reviews regularly for outlets including *Strange Horizons*, *The Los Angeles Review of Books*, *See the Elephant*, *Ginger Nuts of Horror*, and elsewhere. He has co-produced award-winning short films with his ex-wife, the Hungarian filmmaker Lilla Bán. He is an active member of the BDSM community and an occasional contributor to *Skin Two*. He is also official clan poet of Clan Mackintosh.

www.paulstjohnmackintosh.com

www.ingramcontent.com/pod-product-compliance
Lightning Source LLC
Chambersburg PA
CBHW031033190726
48286CB00003BA/1156